The author and publishers would
like to thank the animals at Mudchute and all their friends,
George, Clare, Carol and Michelle, St Luke's School and Cubitt
Town School, and everyone else who helped to produce the book.

First published in Great Britain 1984 by
Hamish Hamilton Children's Books
Garden House, 57–59 Long Acre, London WC2E 9JZ

British Cataloguing in Publication Data
Bennett, Olivia
A farm in the city
823' 914[J] PZ7
ISBN 0-241-11202-8
Printed in Great Britain by
Cambus Litho Ltd. East Kilbride

A FARM IN THE CITY

Olivia Bennett
Photographs by Christopher Cormack

Hamish Hamilton
London

It is early morning at Mudchute Farm. George is milking Maggie the goat. Michelle watches Maggie eat her oats and bran. As long as Maggie has some breakfast to munch, she will stay still.

Michelle starts to milk Annie.
'Pull with one hand and then with the other,' says George.

George and Michelle live in London's dockland. And so do Maggie, Annie and all the other animals at Mudchute! For Mudchute is right in the middle of the warehouses, factories and housing estates of the Isle of Dogs. Its green fields cover a huge mound of earth which was dredged out of the Millwall Docks over a hundred years ago.

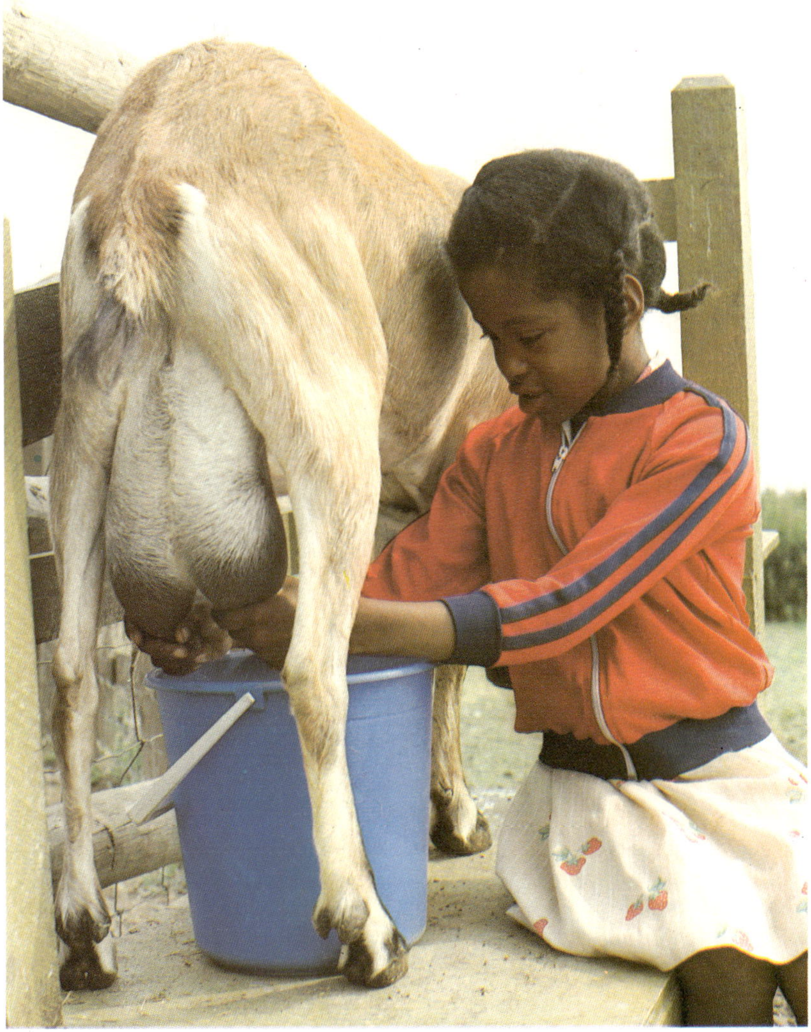

Seven years ago, some local people got together to turn Mudchute into a park and a farm. Today, it is home to horses, cattle, sheep, goats, donkeys, geese, ducks, guinea pigs, rabbits and honey bees.

Mudchute has a lot of visitors. People come to enjoy the open space. Others help to work on the farm. Schools come to learn about the animals. George, Michelle, Carol and Clare spend as much time there as they can. George takes some of the milk to feed Paul the calf.

Carol and Clare carefully strain the rest of the milk through a filter. Then they pour it into small plastic bags. The farm sells goat's milk, cheese and yoghurt.

Then Carol fetches
the hens' new-
laid eggs.
These are sold too.

The next job is to put the goats out to graze. Clare, George and Michelle push, pull and shove but whatever they do the goats seem to want to go in the opposite direction.
'Last time I took Maggie for a walk – she took me!' says Clare.

This morning it is George's turn to clean out the guinea pigs. Clare and Michelle hold the babies while he shovels out the dirty straw. 'They are so wriggly. They won't stop struggling and squeaking.' 'If you hold them close to your chest, they keep still,' says Clare.

Clare and Carol are coming to Mudchute with their class tomorrow. They are quite excited because they will be able to show their friends how well they know all the animals.

The next afternoon Clare and Carol come with their class to Mudchute. Their teacher, Janet, lets everyone run around the fields. Most of them live in tall blocks of flats without much space to play.

'All right, everyone. Now it is time for a little work,' says Janet. 'We are going to see Paul. He is only two weeks old. Don't make a lot of noise or you will frighten him.'
Paul looks a bit wobbly and sleepy at first. Clare holds him so that Lennie can measure his girth. Lennie puts his hands right round Paul's middle.

Then Thomas measures Paul's head. He spreads his hands out with the thumbs touching.
'Oooh! Clare's hand is disappearing into Paul's mouth.'
'He has licked my hand quite clean,' says Clare in surprise.
Another local school has adopted Paul. Each time they visit him, they will measure how much he has grown.

Then the class go to say hello to Brian. Brian is the calf they adopted. He was as small as Paul then, but he is ten months old now. They write him letters and once Brian came to visit them at school. They learnt all sorts of things about cattle and why they have four stomachs.

Janet shows Lornette how to listen to Brian's stomachs.
'It sounds like thunder in there. It makes my ears go all tingly,' says Lornette. 'I was a bit scared because Brian kept walking about.'

Meanwhile Carol has gone to help John. John looks after most of the school groups who come to Mudchute. Today he is going to show them how to clip the wool off a sheep.

‘Do sheep bite?’ asks Donna anxiously.
‘It is quite safe,’ explains John. ‘She is just very hot and she doesn’t like being pulled about and sat on. Imagine you were a sheep and this was happening to you! Hold her still so that I don’t snip off her tail by mistake.’
Janet times John to see how long it takes. ‘Nine minutes exactly!’

Kate shows them how the wool can be used to make clothes. 'Did you feel the wool as it came off the sheep? It is fluffy and a bit oily. If you pull it, it just comes apart. Now twist the wool a little. It gets much stronger, doesn't it? Twisting the wool on a spinning wheel makes it strong enough for knitting and weaving.'

Scott tries carding the wool. 'If you comb it very gently, it makes all the hairs go in the same direction. Carding is done before spinning.'

Janet divides the class into two groups. She takes one down to the stream at the edge of the farm. It is called the Newtie because so many newts live in it.

Some of the children have pond dippers. Janet shows Daniel and the others how to catch some of the different insects which live in the Newtie.

'I've found a water boatman and a water spider,' says Daniel. They look at them through a magnifying glass.

Carol and Ricky are using 'pooters' to catch tiny insects crawling on blades of grass. A pooter is a small pot with two hollow tubes sticking out. They put the end of one tube over an insect and suck hard through the other one. The insect is sucked down the tube into the pot. They have to be very patient and careful to do this.
'I've caught a greenfly, some tiny spiders and a wood-louse,' says Ricky.

Meanwhile John and the others look at wild flowers.
'Use your noses,' says John. 'Which flowers smell sweetest? This is elderflower. Take a good sniff. What does it smell of? You can make jam and wine from its berries.'
'Clover smells nicer,' says Clare. 'The bees like it a lot. It smells a bit like honey.'

'Teatime,' says John. 'We'll have our picnic at the top of the Mudchute.'

From the top they can see the River Thames curling round the Isle of Dogs. Some of them can see where they live. They can hear the clanking and banging of the factories and docks.
The donkeys come so close that they almost eat someone's tea.
Before the children go home, they run races up and down the Mudchute.
'I'm glad we saw Brian again,' Scott tells John.
'I liked seeing the sheep having a haircut best,' says Keeley.

The next afternoon a different John comes to Mudchute. He looks after the beehives. It is a hot, thundery day.
'The bees don't like this weather. They may be a bit bad-tempered.'
'Can we watch?' George and Carol are at Mudchute again!
'As long as you wear beekeepers' hats and gloves and stand at a distance.'
John takes off the outer layers of the hive. Inside there may be as many as 80,000 bees. Each hive can produce about 50 kilograms of honey a year.

John is going to collect some honey. He puffs some smoke into the hive. It makes the bees confused and easier to deal with. Later he shows George and Carol how to do this.

He pulls out a honeycomb from the centre of the hive. Some honey drips off. Another frame shows a new wax comb being built. Then John finds the queen. There is only one in a hive. She can lay as many as 3,000 eggs in one day.

The farm sells the honey. They also sell duck and goose eggs, sheep's wool and horse manure. There are eight horses and ponies at Mudchute. The riding lessons are very popular. Lindy, the instructor, has started a show jumping team. Some of her riders are beginning to win prizes at gymkhanas.

The blacksmith is a regular visitor to Mudchute. While Lindy holds Poppy, he takes off the old shoes. He trims Poppy's nails with a large file. Usually he heats the new shoe so that it sinks into the nail. It does not hurt but Poppy gets very nervous when she smells the smoke.

So this morning the blacksmith's mate measures the shoe against her foot. Then he hammers the cold metal into shape on his anvil. Lindy keeps Poppy still while the blacksmith fits her with four new shoes.

Mudchute's cattle win prizes too. One was champion of the Isle of Dogs Agricultural Show. Many local shows and events take place on the green open spaces of Mudchute.
Patrick lives around the corner from the farm. He spends as much time there as he can. He helps prepare the cattle for shows. He washes Black Beauty's coat and dries and brushes it until it shines.

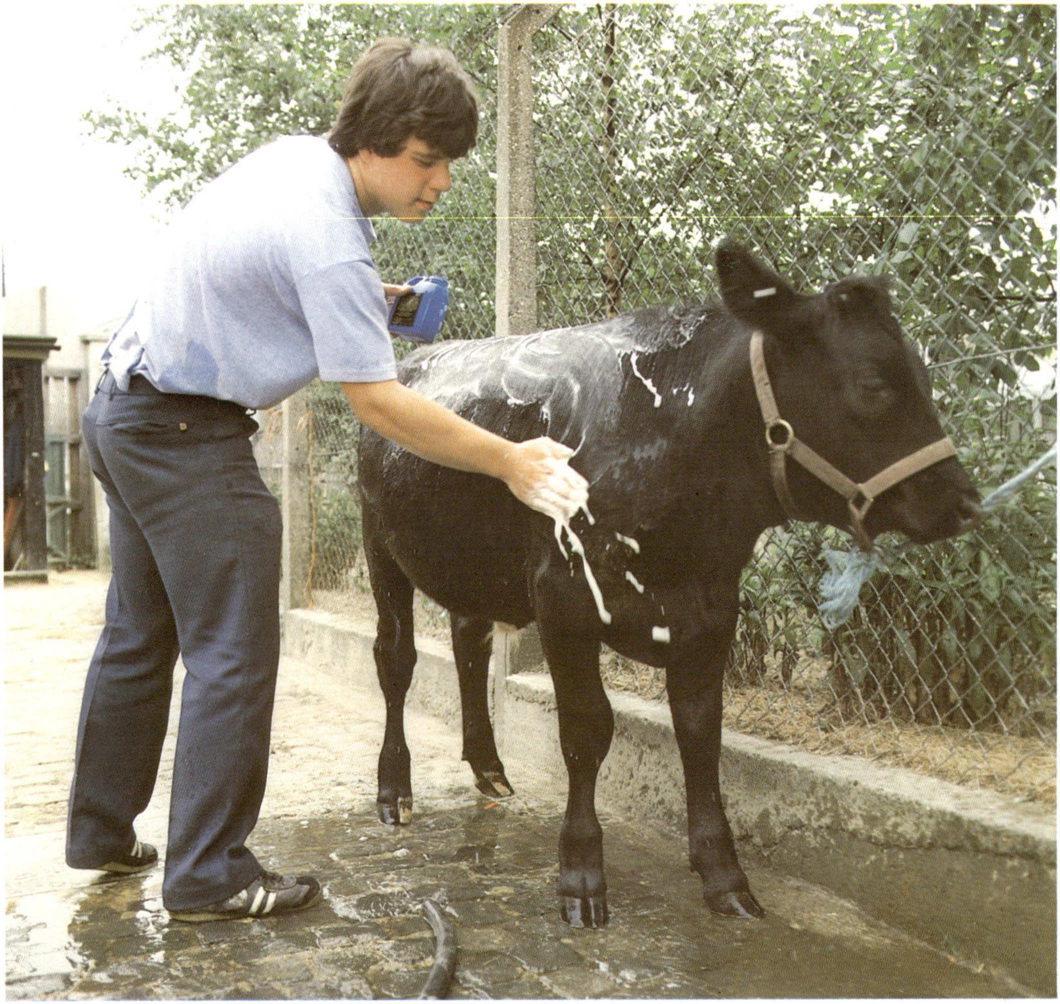

Sometimes the cattle and sheep raised at Mudchute have to be sold. One day Carol, George, Clare and Michelle went to market with Mike, the farm manager. They had to get up early to help him load the van. There was a lot of banging and scuttling in the van when the fifteen lambs were all inside.

When they got to Chelmsford market a man wrote down how much each lamb weighed.

The children stayed with the lambs until the auctioneer came to sell them. They all felt rather quiet and sad when they had to say goodbye to the lambs. So Mike took them off to explore the rest of the market.

When they got back to Mudchute, the animals were being fed and put away for the night.
'I'll help you hose down the van,' said George.

The goats were being as difficult as always! The children helped Mike put them in their pens and said goodnight to Paul and Brian. Paul watched them shut the farm gates and go home. Then he and the other animals at Mudchute settled down for another night.

City farms in England, Scotland and Wales

To find out if there is a city farm near you, contact –

The National Federation of City Farms,
The Old Vicarage,
66 Fraser Street,
Bedminster,
Bristol BS3 4LY.
(Tel: Bristol 660663)

Please enclose a stamped, self-addressed envelope.

An up-to-date list of city farms can also be found in the latest issue of *City Farm News* which is published four times a year.

The address of the farm in this book is:
Mudchute Farm
Pier Street
London E14